CAPTAIN AWESOME TAKES FLIGHT

By STAN KIRBY
Illustrated by GEORGE O'CONNOR

LITTLE SIMON

New York   London   Toronto   Sydney   New Delhi

 LITTLE SIMON

An imprint of Simon & Schuster Children's Publishing Division • 1230 Avenue of the Americas, New York, New York 10020 • First Little Simon paperback edition May 2017 • Copyright © 2017 by Simon & Schuster, Inc. • All rights reserved, including the right of reproduction in whole or in part in any form. • LITTLE SIMON is a registered trademark of Simon & Schuster, Inc., and associated colophon is a trademark of Simon & Schuster, Inc. • For information about special discounts for bulk purchases, please contact Simon & Schuster Special Sales at 1-866-506-1949 or business@simonandschuster.com. • The Simon & Schuster Speakers Bureau can bring authors to your live event. For more information or to book an event contact the Simon & Schuster Speakers Bureau at 1-866-248-3049 or visit our website at www.simonspeakers.com. • Designed by Jay Colvin. • The text of this book was set in Little Simon Gazette.
Manufactured in the United States of America 0317 MTN
10 9 8 7 6 5 4 3 2 1
This book has been cataloged with the Library of Congress.
ISBN 978-1-4814-9442-7 (hc)
ISBN 978-1-4814-9441-0 (pbk)
ISBN 978-1-4814-9443-4 (eBook)

Table of Contents

CHAPTER 1

The Summer Vacation of Doom

JUNE

By
Eugene

RING! It was the final bell of the final day of school! Summer vacation was about to begin!

"So long, Ms. Beasley!" Eugene McGillicudy cried. He leaped up from his desk at Sunnyview Elementary and raced to clean out his cubby. The whole class was already talking about their summer plans.

"We're going to Wet Wally's Waterworld," said Gil Ditko.

"We're going to Bobby Orwell's Insect and Animal Farm!" Evan Mason said.

"My family's going to the Mystery Pit in Kalamazoo," said Marlo Craven. "It's . . . mysteriously pitty."

"Well, *I'm* going to take surfing lessons," said Meredith Mooney, the pinkest girl at Sunnyview

Elementary. She wore a pink ribbon in her hair that matched her pink skirt, pink socks, and even pinker shoes.

"*You're* going surfing?" Eugene asked, surprised.

"Yes, Pukegene," Meredith said. "My surfboard is the brightest pink *ever*, and so is my wet suit."

Eugene was joined by his

friends Sally Williams and Charlie Thomas Jones. "No superhero camp this summer, Eugene?" Sally asked.

"Not this summer," Eugene replied. "I guess I'm going to stay in plain, old Sunnyview."

"My parents are sending me to music camp for a whole month," Charlie said. "I'm going to learn to play the clarinet. Or the tuba. Or the drums, even!"

"And I'm going to soccer camp

for a month too!" Sally said. She pulled a soccer ball out of her cubby and attempted to spin it on her finger. It bounced to the ground.

Eugene was about to hand the ball back to Sally, but he stopped himself. "Wait a minute...," he said. "So *you're* gone for a month and *you're* gone for the same month?!"

This was going to be just like
that time in *Super Dude's Summer
Dude Annual No. 1* when the Dude
team split up because of the diabol-
ical summer weather plans of the
Heat Waver.

What's that you say? You've
never heard of Super Dude? Have

you been living under the largest rock on the planet? Or are you just dizzy from running laps on one of the spinning rings of Saturn? Super Dude is simply the greatest superhero ever and the star of hundreds

of just as great comic books. Eugene, Sally, and Charlie were such big fans that they created their own secret superhero identities: Captain Awesome, Supersonic Sal, and Nacho Cheese Man. Together, they formed the Sunnyview Superhero Squad.

But with two-thirds of the Squad on summer vacation, could this be—GASP! CHOKE! GASP!—the *end* of the Sunnyview Superhero Squad?!

"We'll be back in a month, Eugene," Charlie said.

"But evil never takes a break in Sunnyview!" Eugene replied. "There's Mr. Drools from the Howling Paw Nebula! Dr. Yuck Spinach will be free of the school cafeteria any second now. Queen Stinkypants lives in my house! Who will protect the zoo? Or the comic book store at the mall?"

"Don't worry," Charlie said. "We have one last end-of-the-school-year meeting at the clubhouse tonight!"

"And you'll be fine," Sally assured Eugene. "After all, you *are* Captain Awesome."

Eugene stood in his heroic superhero pose, fist pointed toward the sky. "You're right. I am just *one* superhero, but I am *Captain Awesome*! And I will find a way to protect Sunnyview until your return!" he proclaimed.

CHAPTER 2

Suurrrpprriiise!

By
Eugene

I have some news for you, Eugene!" Eugene's mom said excitedly. She was waiting at the front door when Eugene and his dad arrived home.

"Is summer canceled?" Eugene guessed. "Are aliens coming to finally take Queen Stinkypants back to her home planet?" He pointed to his baby sister, who drooled and shook her rattle.

"Maybe a volcano—*BOOM!*—has
destroyed both soccer camp *and*
music camp, and Sally and Charlie
get to stay in Sunnyview?"

Eugene's mom laughed. "Those are good guesses, but no. It has something to do with our family. . . ."

"Oh, I get it," Eugene realized. "Dad has permanent brain freeze from all the chocolate peanut butter ice cream he's been eating for dessert? And now I have to take over his job at work?"

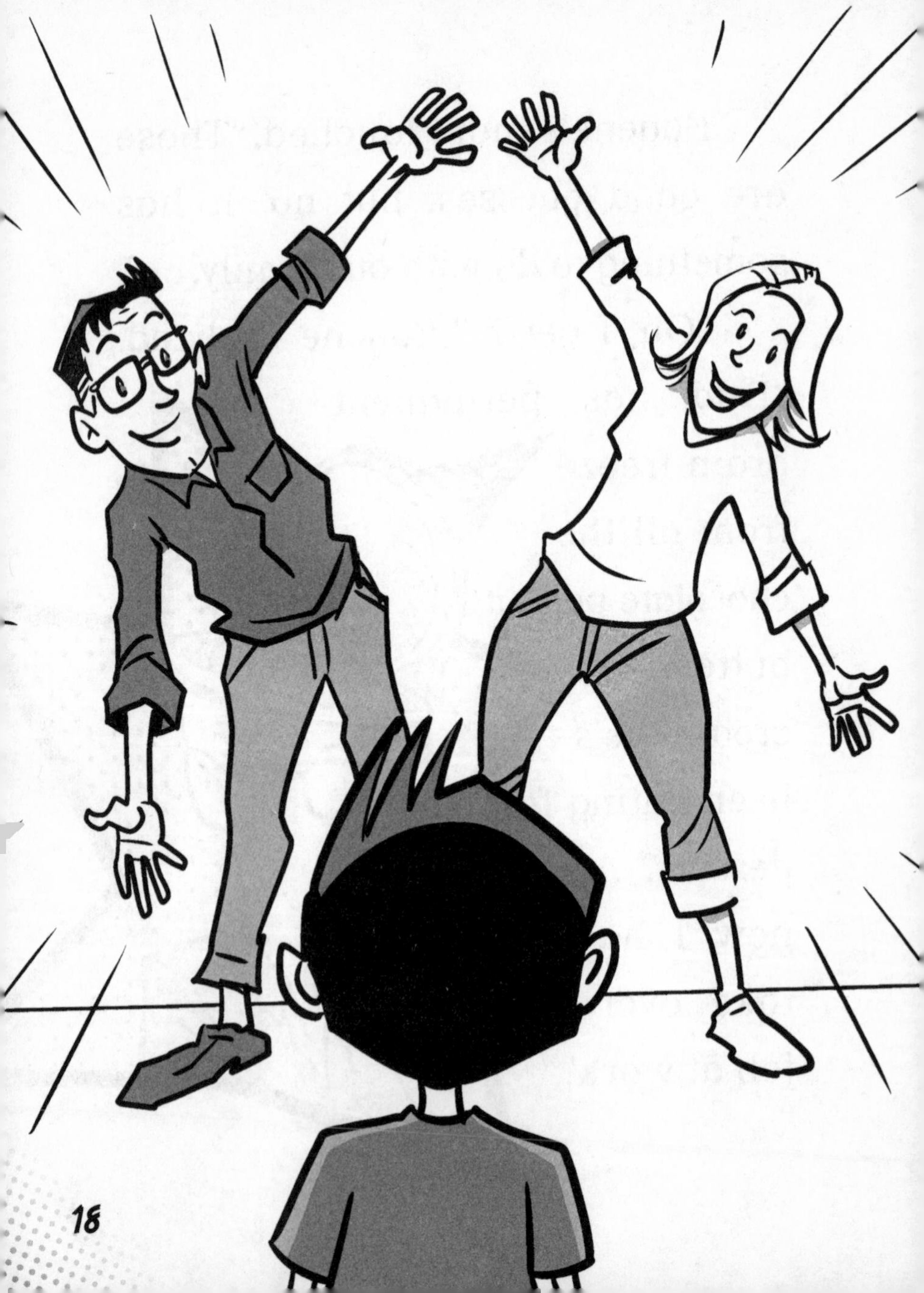

"Not quite," said Eugene's dad. "The surprise is . . ."

"We're going on vacation!" Eugene's mom said. "We will be leaving for the airport first thing in the morning!"

EEP!

EEK!

AAH!

Eugene was speechless. Airport? Airport? *Airport?* His mind raced.

Eugene had never been to the airport! He'd never flown on a plane! All he could think about was

Super Dude No. 19, when Super Dude fought the Sky Pirates and had them walk the cloud plank at 35,000 feet!

Later that day Eugene, Charlie, and Sally were in the clubhouse.

"I'm going to fly!" Eugene burst out. "In the sky! In an airplane!"

"That's so cool!" Charlie said.

"Where are you going?" Sally asked.

Eugene thought for a minute. "I—I forgot to ask! I don't know!"

"Maybe they're taking you to the moon, to fight the Moon King and win back Earth's greatest cheese!" Charlie suggested.

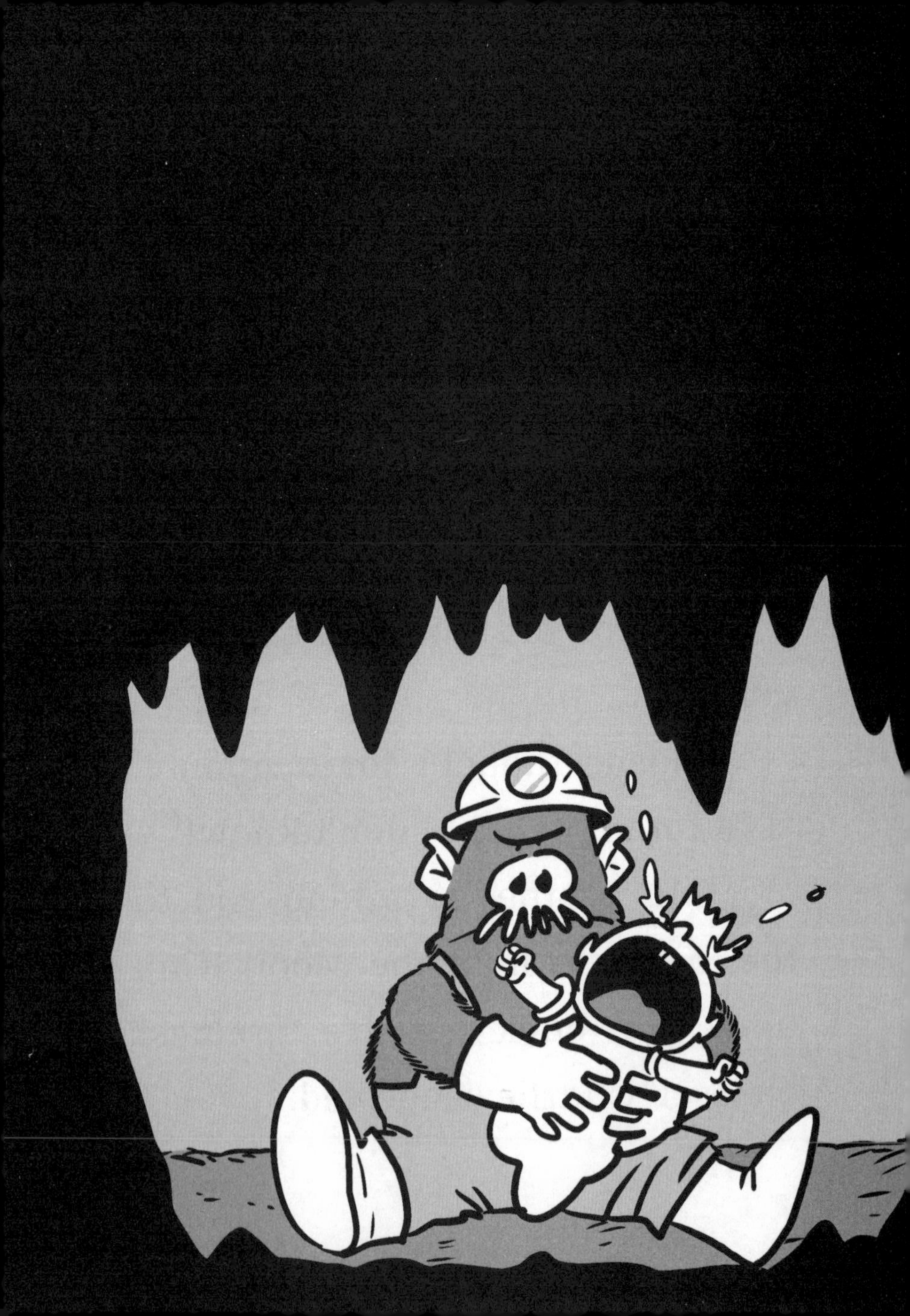

"Or you could be going to the center of the Earth to rescue Prince Crybaby from the evil Mole Master!" Sally replied.

"Wait a minute," Eugene said. "Those are all places from Super Dude's comic books!

"Well, sure!" Sally said. "But that would make your trip *soooo* awesome!"

"I was worried about fighting evil here in Sunnyview, but this is our big chance!" Eugene said. "We can *all* fight evil in new places around the world!"

"If any villain tries to ruin my music camp, I can take care of them with the power of canned cheese," Charlie said.

"And if a villain tries to spoil my soccer camp, I'll run around them so fast with my super speed

that they'll get dizzy and fall over,"
Sally said.

Eugene thought for a moment,
then had a realization. "How can *I*
be ready to fight evil if I don't even
know where I'm going?"

"A superhero should always be prepared," Sally said.

Charlie took out a can of jalapeño cheese and blasted a squirt of it into his mouth. "Mmmhmm!"

"Right!" Eugene agreed. "I'll take my brain, my superhero suit, and my Awesome-Sense. That way I'll be ready for anything!"

CHAPTER 3

Let's Take a Trip into Danger!

By
Eugene

Super Dude escaped from the lava pit of the not-so-fantastic Dr. Fantastic and raced to his private jet, *Super Dude One*. Super Dude revved the engine for takeoff. It coughed and sputtered like Super Cat with a super hairball. The engine started, but before Super Dude could take off, there was a knock on the door. That's right. A knock. Then another one.

KNOCK! KNOCK!

"It's Dr. Fantastic!" Super Dude cried. "He's trying to get in the old-fashioned way— with a terrible knock-knock joke! Maybe he's not so fantastic after all!"

KNOCK! KNOCK!

The knocks got louder and louder until . . .

"Eugene? Wake up!"

Eugene jumped out of his bed and rubbed his eyes.

"Go away, Dr. Fantastic! And take your evil pit of lava with you!" Eugene cried.

"Dr. Fantastic? I like that much better than plain old 'Dad'!" said a voice outside the door.

"Dad?" Eugene said as he opened the bedroom door in surprise. "What are you doing here?"

"It's almost time to go to the airport!" his dad replied cheerfully. "Grab your stuff and come downstairs!"

Eugene checked his Super Dude suitcase one last time to make sure his Captain Awesome suit and gear were safely packed. He zipped up the suitcase and got dressed. Then, with his secret superhuman strength, he carried his suitcase down the stairs.

Once the car was loaded, the McGillicudy family piled in. Eugene's mom and dad were in the front. Queen Stinkypants was in her car seat next to Eugene.

*It's only a matter of time before
she blasts me with a double-diaper
attack,* Eugene thought.

Then Eugene had an even more
terrible thought. What if his parents

were taking them to the world's
largest knitting and yarn festival?

Or some place where they didn't serve macaroni and cheese? Or Stinktown, the place for evil babies like the Diaper Dinosaur and the Chunky Barf Brothers and Queen Stinkypants?!

But before long, the motion of the car was rocking Eugene gently to sleep. Even superheroes need a nap when they wake up early in the morning to drive to the airport and fly to a secret location they hope isn't filled with evil and badness!

CHAPTER 4

Underwear Saves the Day

By
Eugene

We're here!" Eugene's dad said. "Sunnyview International Airport!" He pulled the car over to the curb just as an airplane flew down the runway.

Eugene pressed his face against the car window to watch the plane take off and disappear into the clouds.

"I'll go park the car and meet you at security," Eugene's dad said to the rest of the family. He unloaded the suitcases from the car and set them on the sidewalk. Eugene reached for his, but someone else was already grabbing the handle.

WHOA! WHAT?! "UNHAND MY SUITCASE, VILLAIN!" Eugene cried out, then tried to grab his suitcase from the baggage handler.

The baggage
handler grabbed
back. Eugene pulled again. The
suitcase flew from the baggage
handler's hands. Eugene fell backward, tripped on the curb, and
bounced right into the open trunk
of his car.

A flight attendant walked past and saw Eugene sitting in the trunk. She giggled. "That's the funniest thing I've seen all day," she said. "Are you okay?"

Eugene nodded as he climbed out of the car.

"Hope you have a nice trip," the flight attendant said as she went inside the airport.

"Your suitcase will be okay, Eugene," his mom said. We're just checking our luggage here so they can load it onto the plane. We'll pick it up again when the plane lands."

"But . . . but . . ." Eugene had to think fast. All his Captain Awesome gear was in his suitcase, including his suit. Eugene looked at the baggage

handler, then his mother. His mother looked at the baggage handler and then at Eugene. The baggage handler didn't know where to look.

"You know what, Eugene? If you promise to carry your suitcase by yourself, you can take it on the plane with us," his mom said with a wink. "How does that sound?"

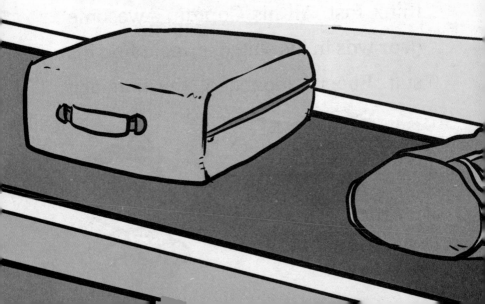

Like a victory for justice! Eugene thought. He smiled at his mom and picked up his suitcase.

A little while later, Eugene's dad met them at the security check. He put his suitcase on the conveyor belt that led to the X-ray machine. "You're up, Eugene."

Eugene watched his dad's suitcase disappear into the metal machine.

"But what if this machine doesn't give me my suitcase back, Dad?" he asked. *Or worse,* Eugene thought, *what if the machine is a power-sucking device that sucks all*

the power from my Awesome suit?!

"It comes out at the other end," Eugene's dad replied. "We'll pick it up again after we go through the metal detector."

Slowly, carefully, Eugene lifted his suitcase onto the conveyor belt. Eugene watched the conveyor belt carry away

the suitcase. It was going . . . going . . .
gone. Eugene noticed that the security guards were smiling.

They know something! Eugene
thought.

He leaped for his suitcase.
"Come back!" he cried. But he was
too late.

"It'll be okay, Eugene," his dad
said. "Now it's our turn to go through
the metal detector." He pointed to
the steel archway with a blinking
light on top. Eugene gasped.

"I have to go through . . . THAT?"
he asked.

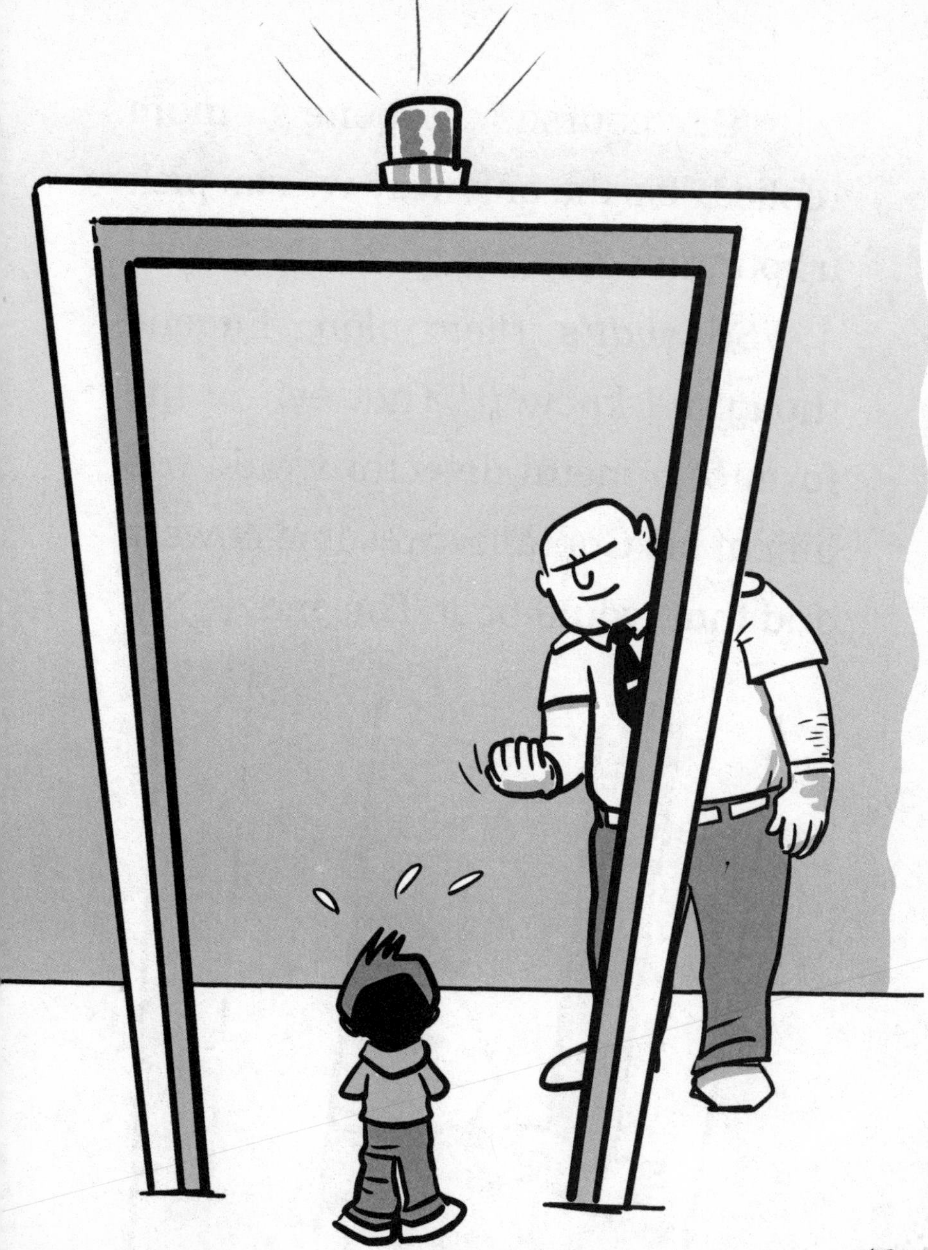

"Of course," Eugene's mom replied. "It's the only way we can pick up our suitcases and get on the plane."

So *that's their plan,* Eugene thought. *I knew it!* That evil in the form of a metal detector would rob him of his Captain Awesome powers and that would be it. The end.

Eugene's dad nudged him. "Go on. We're holding up the line."

Eugene gulped. He inched his way through the metal detector, turning sideways to try to avoid as many of its evil rays as possible.

Once he was through, he saw his suitcase at the end of the conveyor belt, just like his dad said. He rushed to it and reached for it.

But the big hand of a security guard got there first.

NOT AGAIN!

"Is this your bag, buddy?" he asked. "Random security check."

Random?! In the world of superheroes traveling in secret, nothing is ever random. Except . . . when it's evil. Evil can be very random.

UNZIP!
UNZIP!
MORE UNZIP!

The security guard unzipped
Eugene's suitcase. And his Captain
Awesome suit was sitting RIGHT.
ON. TOP.

Was the security guard about to discover that Eugene was the world's second-greatest superhero? Would his secret identity be a secret no more?!

But Eugene didn't have a chance to cover up his suit. A pair of underwear had stuck to the top of the suitcase. It dropped to the floor.

"What do we have here? Looks like underwear." The security guard picked it up and placed it back in the suitcase. "Can't travel on an

airplane without clean underwear!"
He closed the suitcase and zipped
it. "Have a safe trip."

Eugene breathed a sigh of relief.
He was safe . . . for now.

CHAPTER 5

A Robotic Black Hole Transporter!

By
Eugene

Suitcase in hand, Eugene followed his parents toward the gate.

He looked around as they walked. A woman standing in line to get coffee was dressed in a parka as if it were snowing in the airport, but behind her was a man in shorts wearing a Hawaiian T-shirt. Some people ran toward their planes. Some people walked. Others rode in beeping carts.

Airports, Eugene realized, are like a pile of crayons melted into one giant, colorful glob of people, languages, shops, food, lines, and strange announcements.

This place is just like the Outer Dimensional Space Port from Super Dude's Outer Dimensional Space Port Adventure No. 4, Eugene thought.

"Hop on, Eugene. You're blocking the people behind you," Eugene's dad said.

Eugene looked around. "Hop on what?" he asked.

His dad pointed to the floor.

Eugene looked down.

SHOCK!

The ground was moving!

Eugene wrapped his arms around his dad's leg and held him back. "Don't step on that thing, Dad! It's a Robotic Black Hole Transporter! It'll suck you into a black hole and we'll never get on our plane!"

"I've gotta go change Molly," said Eugene's mom. "I'll be back."

"It's not a black hole-whatever-you-said," Eugene's dad began.

"It just *moves* people through the airport."

"And into a black hole?" Eugene asked, peering past his dad to see if his mom had been sucked into this black hole yet.

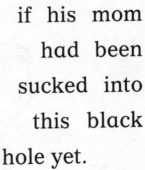

"No black holes. I promise," Eugene's dad replied.

There was no way Eugene was going to ride on some crazy moving walkway without going into full superhero mode. Eugene put his suitcase on the ground, ready to pull out his Captain Awesome outfit. But he accidentally placed the suitcase at the edge of the moving walkway. And it was now *moving away* from him!

Eugene gasped. "I knew this thing was evil!"

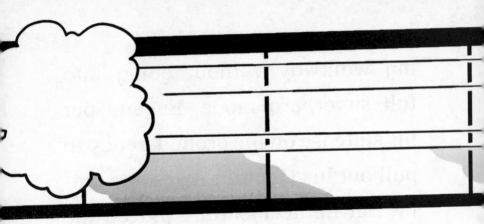

He jumped onto the moving sidewalk to grab his suitcase, but something more unexpected than actually enjoying a plate of asparagus happened . . .

The moving walkway was kind of fun!

A few minutes later, Eugene's mom returned with Molly in a fresh diaper.

"Where's Eugene?" she asked Eugene's dad.

Eugene's dad replied by pointing his thumb back over his shoulder.

"MI-TEEE!" Eugene shouted as he ran back and forth on the moving sidewalk as if it were the greatest amusement park ride in the world.

CHAPTER 6

The Suspicious Pepperoni Slice

By
Eugene

The airport . . . is . . . awesome!
What . . . ride . . . are . . . we going
on . . . next?" Eugene asked, breath-
less from running up and down the
moving sidewalk.

"*Next*," his mom said, "is lunch."

Eugene gave her a thumbs-up.
"Good plan, Mom. All that super
running has given me a super-
hungry tummy."

"So do you guys want salads,

or maybe some veggie burgers?" Eugene's mom asked, scanning the available restaurants.

"Salads?! Veggie burgers?!" Eugene gasped. "Did I run so fast that I teleported to some crazy backward dimension where all the good food was destroyed by a giant volcano and the only

thing left to eat is yucky stuff like salads?"

"I thought we'd eat something healthy," Eugene's mom explained.

"There is nothing healthy about vegetables smashed into hamburger form, Mom!" Eugene frantically explained. "It is one of the five biggest crimes against the yummi- ness of

hamburgers, hot dogs, and cheese fries."

"We could go get pizza," Eugene's dad said, also hoping to avoid the awfulness of lettuce in a bowl for lunch. "That has vegetables *and* fruit on it," he said, giving Eugene a wink.

"That's right!" Eugene said with a gasp. "Because tomatoes are fruit!"

Eugene's mom rolled her eyes. "I'll make you guys a deal. We can get pizza, but you have to have apple slices too."

"Deal!" Eugene blurted out, and raced to stand in line for pizza.

And that's when he saw . . . HER! The flight attendant from check-in was standing in line right in front of Eugene's family!

"Oh! Hello again!" she said to Eugene with a smile. "Where are you going on your summer vacation?"

"You'll never get us to tell you! Never!" Eugene yelled.

"What my son means is that it's a surprise," Eugene's mom cut in, with a slightly embarrassed laugh.

"You know what the best thing about surprises is?" the flight attendant asked Eugene.

"It's that you never know *when* they might happen."

She winked at Eugene's mom, grabbed the last slice of pepperoni pizza, and walked to the tables.

You never know *when* they might happen? What was that supposed to mean?

Eugene wondered about it as he watched the flight attendant eat the last slice of his favorite kind of pizza. And then it hit him like a candy-loving kid swinging at a birthday piñata.

She's planning some type of surprise, thought Eugene. And I'll bet it's an evil surprise! That's why she's always being so nice. It's so I don't see her true evilness!

"I'll be watching you," Eugene whispered as he gave the flight attendant a cold stare.

CHAPTER 7

Delayed by the Fun E. Racer!

By
Eugene

Eugene didn't think it was possible to *ruin* pizza. But the combination of the flight attendant taking the last pepperoni slice and Eugene realizing that she was an agent of evil did exactly that. It ruined his pizza.

Now at their gate, Eugene plopped into his seat in the waiting area and let out a big sigh.

Eugene understood how Super

Dude felt when the Eye Scream Sunday used her evil eye to ruin Super Dude's birthday cake in Super Dude No. 264. It was a good thing that the Banana Splitter was there to help Super Dude knock her all the way to Monday morning.

To take his mind off his super problems, Eugene dug into his suitcase and pulled out a Super Dude comic and the latest Rider Woofson book, *Undercover in the Bow-Wow Club.*

But before Eugene could finish the first page of his book, he heard ...
THE VOICE.
"Welcome to Oceanside Airlines," the crackly voice

sounded over the loudspeaker. "I'm sorry to say that our three p.m. flight from gate thirty-one has been delayed. The new flight time is now four p.m. Thank you for choosing Oceanside Airlines."

Eugene's parents and every-one sitting next to them groaned in

unison at hearing their flight would be delayed.

Delayed?! Eugene thought. He quickly searched the area to see who was making the announcement, and then he saw *her*, holding the microphone in her hand. It was . . .

The same flight attendant!

As the final puzzle piece fell into place, every-thing suddenly made sense. The flight attendant wasn't really a flight attendant at all. She was . . . the evil Fun E. Racer, and she was there to ruin Eugene's vacation!

First she'd laughed when the bag handler tried to take Eugene's suitcase, then she'd taken the last slice of pepperoni pizza, and now

she was making their plane leave one hour late!

It's time to get Awesome!

Eugene grabbed his suitcase.

ZIP!

COSTUME!

HERO TIME!

Captain Awesome hid behind a large piece of luggage and scanned the area. He would have to act fast. If he didn't, who knew how many vacations the Fun E. Racer would ruin! He needed an Awesome Plan of Goodness to counter her Rotten Plan of Badness.

The luggage he was hiding behind had wheels. Perfect! A woman with a poodle was sitting five chairs away. Double perfect! A man eating a hot dog sat next to her. Triple perfect!

Eugene considered his plan.

I'll ride the luggage to the lady with the poodle and grab the dog, because, well, I might need one. Then I'll backflip to the man with the hot dog and snag the leftover mustard packets. I'll grab the hat off the guy across from the hot dog man—no, I'll grab his shoe. No! I'll grab his hat and his shoe!

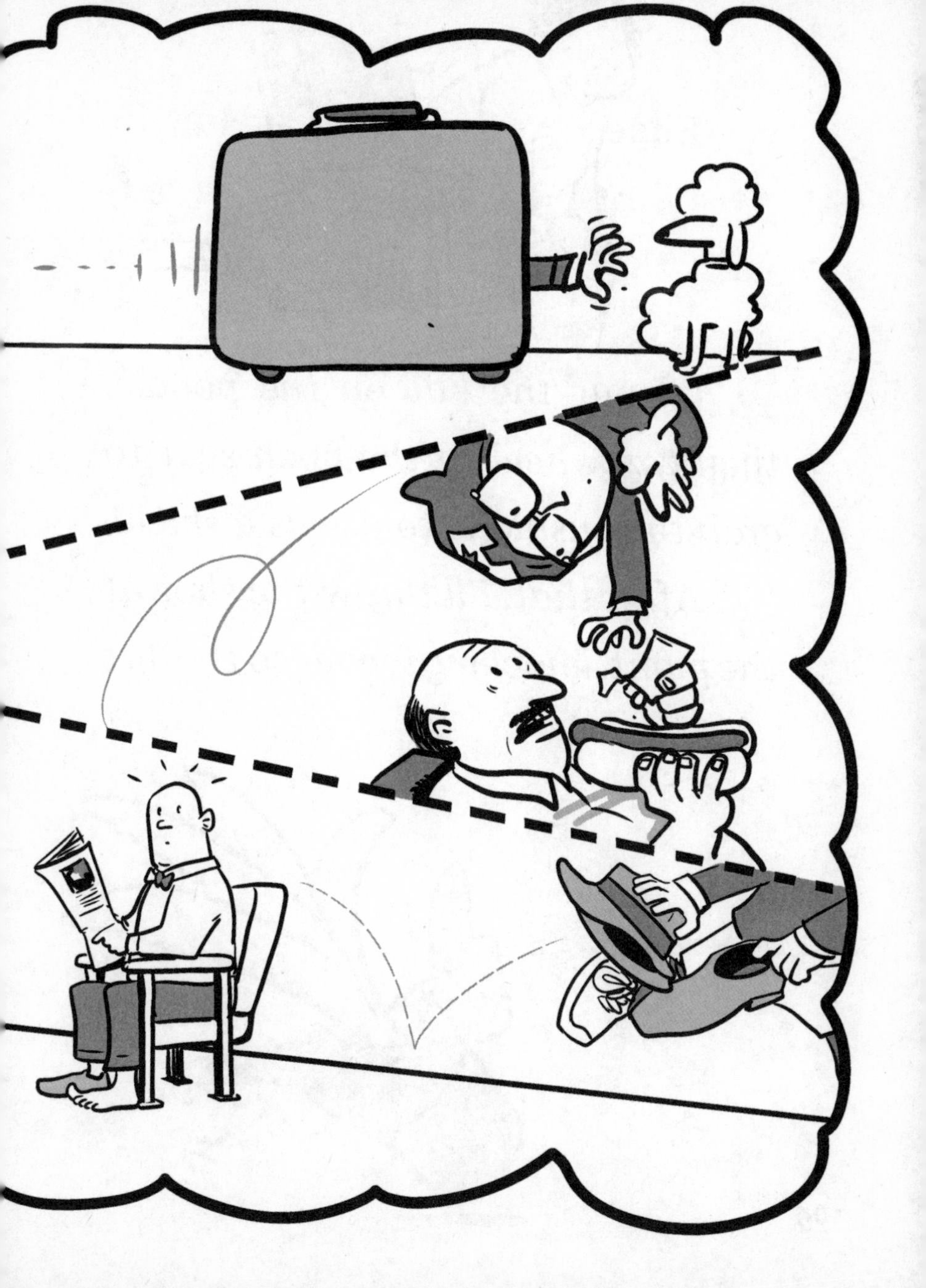

I'll put the hat on the poodle, then cartwheel to the open seat to grab the cushions to use as a shield. After that, I'll throw the shoe at the plant, knocking it over so the dirt

spills into the walkway, which will distract everyone so I can launch the full awesomeness of my Captain Awesome Mustard Packet Poodle-in-a-Hat Attack!

It was go time! There wasn't a moment to lose!

"Who wants sour gummy worms?" Eugene's dad held out a bag of sour goodness.

"Sour gummy worms?!" Captain Awesome jumped from behind the suitcase and looked at the gooey, chewy rainbow-colored worms in his dad's hand.

Well, maybe I have a little time, he thought. *After all, I can't save the world without some superhero fuel.*

CHAPTER 8

Two Captains Are Better Than One

By
Eugene

If there's a more perfect food in the world than sour gummy worms, I sure can't think of it, Captain Awesome thought as he sucked down his last worm. *If only scientists could figure out a way to put them on pizza. . . .*

Filled to the cape with super-hero fuel, Captain Awesome was ready to tackle the forces of badness once more.

BUT WAIT!

The Fun E. Racer was gone!

Arrrrrrgh! I bet she used her Zero-Fun Brain-Control Laser to make my dad offer me gummy worms so I'd be distracted by their gummy yumminess and she could make her escape! Captain Awesome thought.

"Hello for a third time!" came a sudden voice from behind Captain Awesome.

Captain Awesome spun around and found himself cape-to-uniform with the villain herself: the Fun E. Racer!

Captain Awesome grabbed a seat cushion and squished it atop his head. "You won't zap *me* with your Zero-Fun Brain-Control Laser! There's no way you're stopping anyone from going on vacation! Because I'm CAPTAIN AWESOME!"

Eugene struck a dramatic super-hero pose—or at least a pose that was as dramatic as it could be with a seat cushion squished on his head.

"I'm not trying to stop anyone from going anywhere, Captain . . . um . . . Awesome, was it?" The flight attendant paused. "Remember that surprise I told you about at the pizza place? Well, I thought you might like to meet another captain."

Captain Awesome's eyes went wide. *Another* captain? Why would the Fun E. Racer want him to meet another captain? Was this "captain" her bad-guy sidekick? Had this captain come to steal all his sour gummy worms so he'd run out of superhero fuel?

"Nice to meet you, Captain Awesome," a man who was also wearing a uniform said. But unlike the Fun E. Racer, he was wearing a hat. "I'm Captain Cool," he continued.

"Captain Cool? Are . . . are you a superhero or an evil sidekick?" Captain Awesome lifted the seat cushion from his head.

"Um, neither, actually. I'm the captain of the airplane you'll be flying on for your vacation." Captain Cool motioned to a large airplane that was now sitting outside.

Captain Awesome's mouth dropped open faster than Super Dude had dropped the Hater Tot's Hot Potato Bomb in Super Dude No. 62.

"You're the captain of an airplane? A REAL airplane? A big one? That really flies? In the air?" Captain Awesome gasped.

"Yes, yes, yes, yes, and yes," Captain Cool replied. He dug into his pocket and handed Eugene a small pin. "This is for you. And make sure you come say hello to

me once we're in the air. I'll show you around the pilot's cabin."

Captain Cool tipped his hat to Eugene's mom and dad, then headed for the plane.

Eugene looked into his hands.
There sat a pin shaped like a pair
of wings. "Mi-teeeeeee," Captain
Awesome whispered.

"I'm glad you like it," said the Fun E. Racer, who was actually just a flight attendant after all. "Oh! By the way, my name's Sally."

"That's one of my best friend's names!" Captain Awesome cried excitedly.

"Then I've got a feeling we're going to get along just fine," Sally said.

Captain Awesome thought for a moment. Then he glanced up at Sally. "So you weren't trying to stop us from going on vacation?" he asked.

"Of course not!" Sally laughed. "And I really think you'll like where your parents are taking you."

Captain Awesome plopped into

the chair and looked once more
at the pin in his hand. He had his
wings. Now he just needed to fly!

CHAPTER 9

The Best Place on Earth

RIGHT HERE!

By Eugene

CLICK!

With his Captain Awesome outfit neatly folded and tucked back
into his suitcase, Eugene was now
seated on the airplane. He clicked
his seat belt into place.

Sally the flight attendant
passed by and handed him extra
packages of cookies and peanuts.
Eugene thanked her and put his
Super Dude comics into the seat

pocket in front of him. He settled in, ready for his flight to . . .

"Wait . . . where *are* we going?" Eugene suddenly asked.

"To the best place ever!" Eugene's dad answered. "Where's

the *one* place you've been asking to go ever since you started reading Super Dude comics?"

"To Super Dude's Super Dude Satellite that's orbiting Pluto?!" Eugene cried excitedly.

"To the best place ever on *Earth*," Eugene's mom said from the seat behind them.

"WAIT." Eugene gasped. "Are we going to SUPER WORLD?!"

"You got it!" Eugene's dad said.

"Super World! Home to the Mega Bouncy House of Mega Bounciness . . . ," began Eugene.

"And the No Gravity Blaster-tastic Roller Coaster," said Eugene's mom.

"Moooo gaaaaaa pooooooo blllaaarrrrrrgh!" Molly added.

"And don't forget the Super Dude Rocket Racers! And the Super Dude Dudercoaster! And

the Super Dude-A-Whirl! And the
Baron Von Broccoli Barfitorium!
And the Loopinator! And the Drop-
inator! And the Spininator! And
the Flying Leaping Jumpinator!"

"Don't worry, we'll ride them all," Eugene's dad said with a pat on Eugene's shoulder.

Eugene sat back in his seat, flipped open a comic book, and smiled. No, he wasn't smiling because Super Dude was about to deflate the Mega Mondo Balloon Blob and save the world. He was smiling because he knew this summer was going to be greater than great and better than the best! This summer was going to be . . .

MI-TEE!

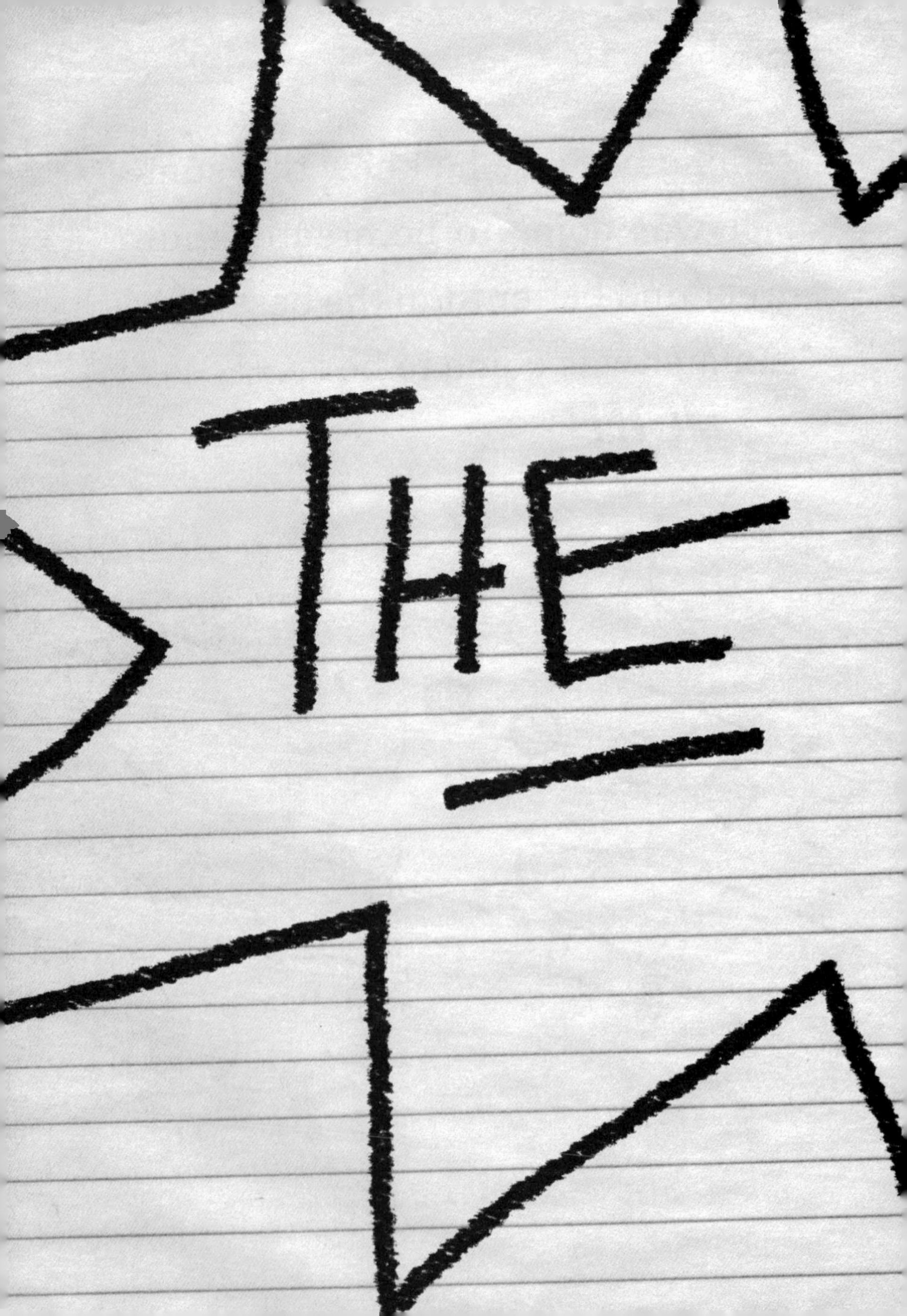
THE

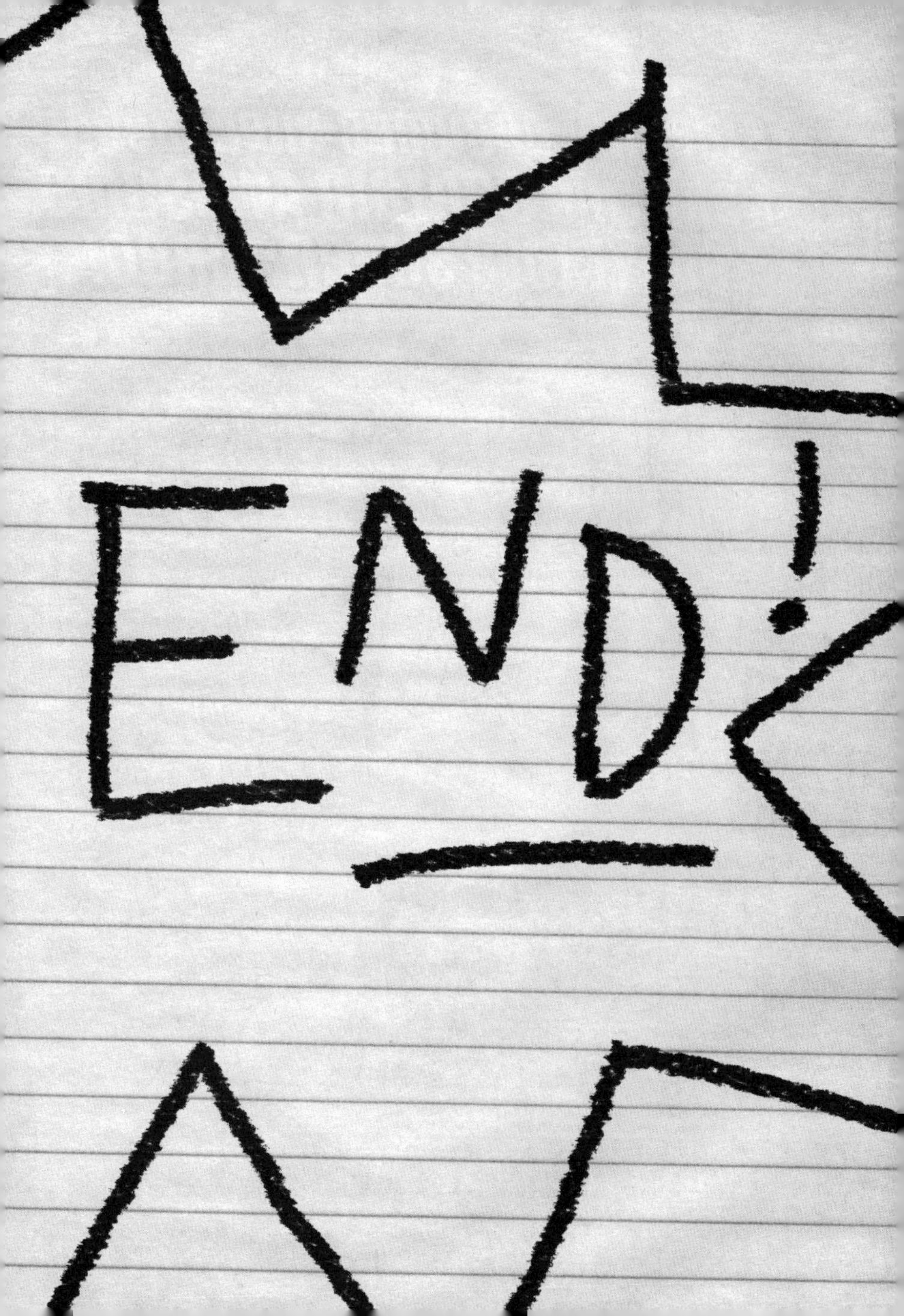
END!

SIDEKICK BECOMES SUPERHERO!
IF YOU LIKE CAPTAIN AWESOME, YOU'LL LOVE SUPER TURBO!

1
SUPER TURBO
SAVES THE DAY!
BY LEE KIRBY
ILLUSTRATED BY GEORGE O'CONNOR

2
SUPER TURBO
VS. THE FLYING NINJA SQUIRRELS
BY LEE KIRBY
ILLUSTRATED BY GEORGE O'CONNOR

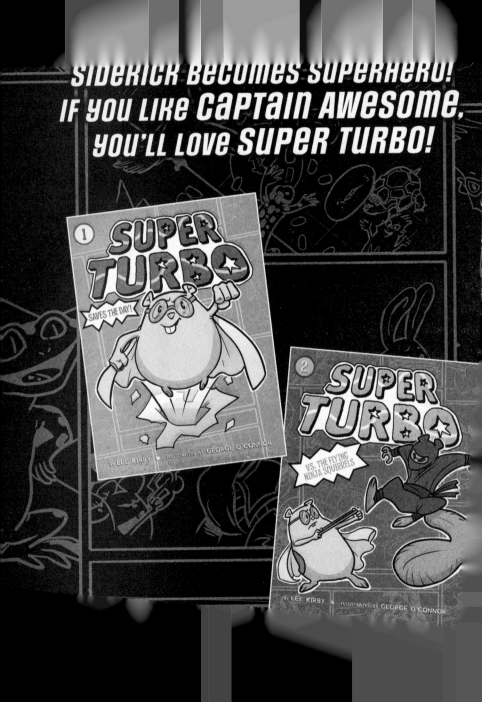

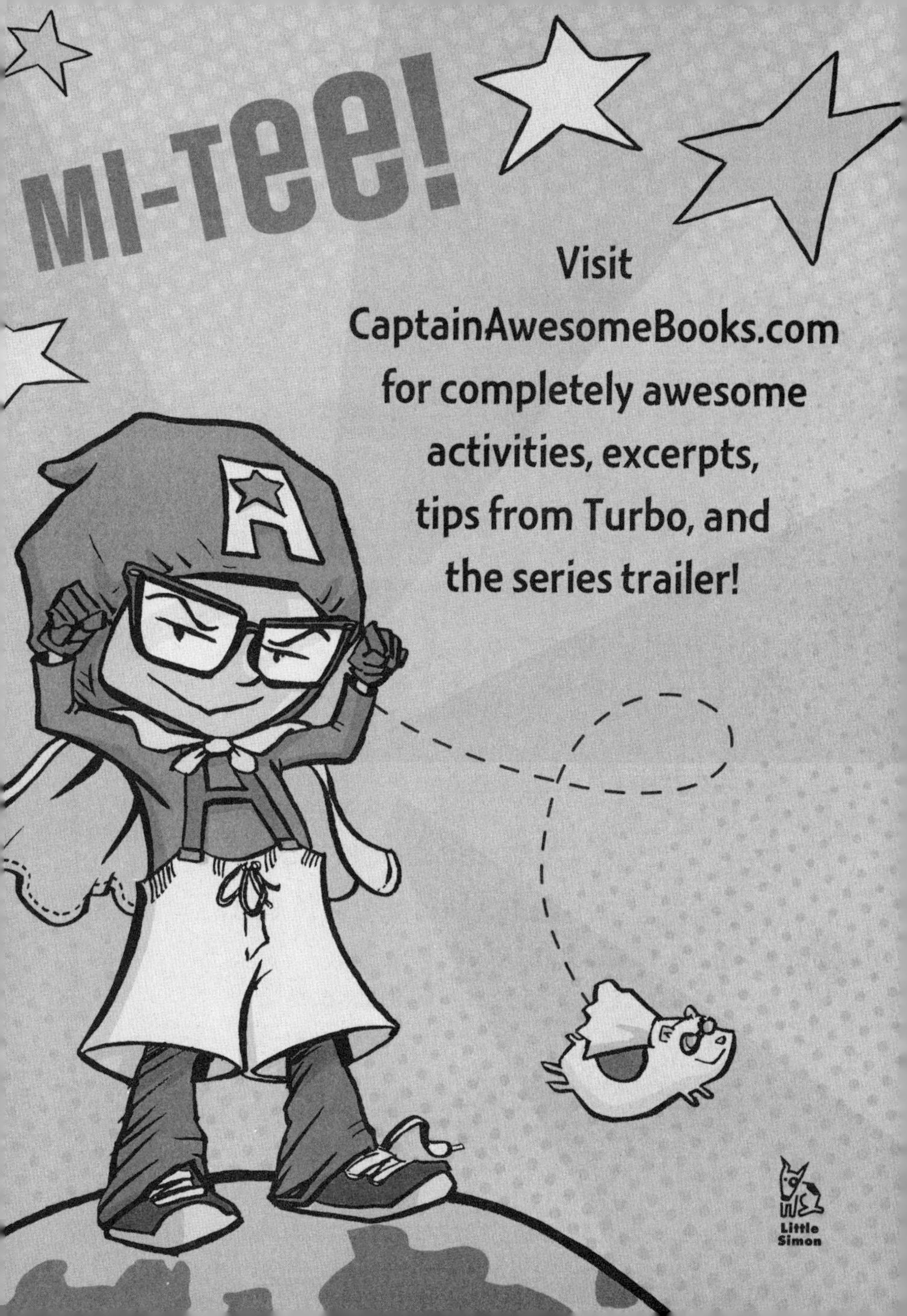
MI-TEE!
Visit
CaptainAwesomeBooks.com
for completely awesome
activities, excerpts,
tips from Turbo, and
the series trailer!
Little Simon

Looking for another great book?
Find it
IN THE MIDDLE.

Fun, fantastic books for kids
in the in-be**TWEEN** age.

IntheMiddleBooks.com